S0-BBF-771

For my grandchildren
Thomas, Harry, Ella and Madeleine

Milly, Molly and Jimmy's Seeds

Copyright© Milly Molly Books, 2003

Gill Pittar and Cris Morrell assert the moral right to
be recognized as the author and illustrator of this work.

All rights reserved. No part of this book may be
reproduced or utilized in any form or by any means,
electronic, or mechanical, including photocopying,
recording, or by any information storage or
retrieval system without the prior written permission
of the publisher.

Published by
Milly Molly Books
P O Box 539
Gisborne, New Zealand
email: books@millymolly.com

Printed by Rhythm Consolidated Berhad, Malaysia

ISBN: 1-86972-000-8

10   9   8   7   6   5   4   3   2   1

Milly, Molly
and
Jimmy's Seeds

"We may look different
but we feel the same."

One day Jimmy's desk was empty.

Jimmy wasn't the sort to stay in bed with
a cold or a bump. He wasn't the sort to
stay in bed at all. Jimmy loved school.
He loved being right in the middle
of everything.

But best of all, Jimmy loved growing plants.
He always had something growing in a pot
or a packet of seeds in his pocket.

If Jimmy was sent out of math class for
talking, he always slipped off quietly
to help the gardener.
But Jimmy never missed school.
It was very, very odd.

Jimmy's desk was empty again
the next day...

...and the next.

When his desk was still empty at the end
of the week, Milly and Molly and all
Jimmy's friends were very worried indeed.

It was comforting when Miss Blythe suggested Jimmy was probably sick with the measles or mumps. Everyone expected him to be back at his desk in no time.

Then one morning, Miss Blythe seemed different.
She sat on the small chair in the middle of
the classroom and asked everyone to gather
closely around her.

She explained gently that Jimmy wouldn't be
coming back to school. She said very softly
that Jimmy had been taken to the hospital and
had died peacefully in the night.

Miss Blythe stretched her arms around
everyone and they all cried together.

Miss Blythe didn't mind that they missed
math or spelling.

And no one felt like singing or playing games
at lunch-time.

Miss Blythe was happy just to chat
and listen and give lots of hugs.

It upset Milly and Molly to look at Jimmy's empty desk. But they didn't want Miss Blythe to take it away either.

They decided to put a bunch of flowers
on Jimmy's desk and for a while that helped.
Everyone took part in bringing flowers from
their gardens and they kept Jimmy's bunch
of flowers fresh and beautiful.

When everyone was ready, Jimmy's desk
was taken away.

Milly and Molly very carefully put Jimmy's
books and bits and pieces in a box for his
mother to collect.

Tucked away in the corner of Jimmy's desk,
Milly and Molly had found a packet of seeds
amongst an extraordinary assortment
of pens and pencils.

With Jimmy's mother's blessing, Milly and
Molly planted the seeds in the school garden
on a warm sunny day.

They watered and waited...
...and waited and watered.

On the twelfth day, a row of small green
plants pushed their heads up through the soil.
Every day they slowly grew bigger.
Suddenly, the middle plant grew taller
and taller.

It grew so tall it had to be tied to the fence.

And then miraculously, overnight...

...there stood a great big sunflower with
a round happy face. Milly and Molly and
all Jimmy's friends were delighted.
Jimmy was back again, right in the middle
of everything.